THE SECRET OF THE UNKYARD SHADOW

READ ALL THE

CABIN CREEK MYSTERIES

#1: The Secret of Robber's Cave

#2: The Clue at the Bottom of the Lake

#3: The Legend of Skull Cliff

#4: The Haunting of Hillside School

#5: The Blizzard on Blue Mountain

#6: The Secret of the Junkyard Shadow

THE SECRET OF THE
JUNKYARD SHADOW

by Kristiana Gregory
Illustrated by Patrick Faricy

SCHOLASTIC INC.
New York   Toronto   London   Auckland   Sydney
Mexico City   New Delhi   Hong Kong   Buenos Aires

ISBN-13: 978-0-545-00380-3
ISBN-10: 0-545-00380-6

Text copyright © 2009 by Kristiana Gregory
Illustrations copyright © 2009 by Scholastic Inc.
"David's Map" illustration by Cody Rutty.

12 11 10 9 8 7 6 5 4 3 2 1   9 10 11 12 13 14/0

Printed in the U.S.A.   40

First printing, May 2009

CHAPTERS

1. The Trespasser   1
2. A Big Mess   8
3. KIDS KEEP OUT!!   18
4. A New Shortcut   26
5. A Stern Warning   35
6. The Predicament   42
7. A Dreadful Mistake   51
8. Fort Grizzly Paw   58
9. Another Surprise   68
10. Someone Is Watching   75
11. More Questions   83
12. An Unlikely Friend   89
13. An Important Interview   98
14. A New Suspect   106
15. A Personal Matter   114
16. The Ol' Switcheroo   120

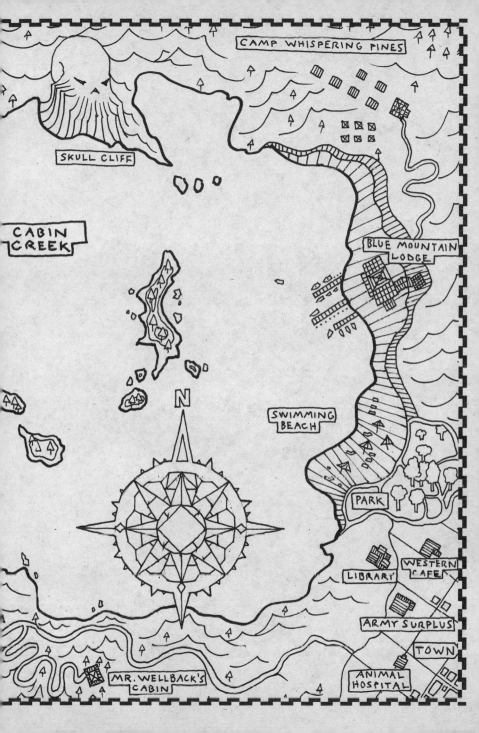

1

The Trespasser

The lookout tower swayed in the wind. It was actually an oak tree, the tallest one on Lost Island. High in its branches, twelve-year-old Jeff Bridger perched with his binoculars.

The view was spectacular. Though it was spring, the mountains in the distance were still white with snow. The surrounding forests were pale green with new growth. Jeff scanned the lake and its far shore that touched the marina.

His gaze then followed the road that led past the café and the library.

At the edge of town, he focused on the junkyard.

"There he is again," Jeff said to his cousin, Claire, who sat beside him on their homemade platform.

"I see him, too," she said. Claire Posey was nine. Her red hair blew around her face as she looked through her binoculars. She could read the danger signs on the barbed-wire fence. One showed a skull and crossbones with the word POISON. Another sign said: *NO KIDS ALLOWED, EVER, AND THAT'S FINAL.*

"Is he carrying that suitcase again?" called David from the base of the tree. He was Jeff's younger brother, age ten, and today was in charge of delivering snacks to their lookout tower. The children's three dogs were wagging their tails as David fed them crackers from the torn bag in his hand.

"Yep, same as yesterday," Claire yelled down to him. "Wearing overalls and boots. Still can't see his face. He's hunched over in the shadows."

A creaking rope rubbed against a branch as it rolled upward and over a pulley. A bucket soon appeared, clunking against the platform.

"Got it!" Jeff cried, leaning down. A lock of his brown hair fell over his eyes. He removed a carton of orange juice and the crackers. Claire made room on her seat for David, who climbed up to join them. The three zipped their sweatshirts against the cold air.

The cousins loved being on Lost Island, where their secret clubhouse was hidden in the woods. That morning, they had beached their canoe in one of the quiet coves. School was out for spring vacation. Now that the ice had melted off the lake, they planned to paddle over from their cabins as often as possible.

"I heard the junkyard guy lives there in an old car with some pet tarantulas," Jeff said. He took a swig of juice and passed the carton to Claire.

"We should investigate," she replied. She took a swig and passed it to David.

"Definitely!" the younger boy agreed. His blond hair was unruly in the wind. He gulped the juice, which spilled onto his shirt. Mopping it with his sleeve, he said, "I've always wanted to look around that place. I like junk. Wonder what kind of danger is in there."

"Maybe his tarantulas bite," said Jeff. "That's why he doesn't want kids around."

Claire finished a cracker, then picked up her binoculars. "And maybe they're poisonous. Hey, guys, check this out."

The brothers focused their lenses. They could see the man putting small objects into the suitcase. He strapped it shut, then heaved it over the fence. It landed in a puff of dirt. The man looked around and behind him, as if hoping no one was watching. Then he crawled under the barbed wire, grabbed the suitcase, and ran through the woods.

The children set their binoculars down.

"If that's the owner, why didn't he go out the gate?" Claire asked.

"And it's weird that he put stuff in a suitcase," said David.

Jeff nodded. "Yeah. Whoever this guy is, I bet he's doing something he shouldn't."

2

A Big Mess

The cousins climbed down from their lookout tower.

Tessie, the old yellow Lab, led them to their clubhouse, which the children had named Fort Grizzly Paw. It was an abandoned log cabin with a missing wall. A pine tree had rooted itself in the dirt floor and was growing up through the roof. The kids decorated the branches as if it were a strange Christmas tree,

hanging up their sweatshirts, canteens, whistles, and walkie-talkies.

"So, guys, what's next?" Claire began. She spread a blanket for the two little dogs: Yum-Yum, her white poodle, and Rascal, the black Scottish terrier. Tessie curled up on an old, soft sleeping bag.

The children liked to conduct their meetings at their table. It was a large round stump they had found in the forest and rolled into the cabin. Its surface bore hatchet marks from someone who had chopped wood on it long ago. David liked to draw here. He took out his notebook and began sketching the figure with the suitcase. He labeled it, *Shadowy guy in junkyard.*

Jeff said, "I think we should go look for clues, even though kids aren't allowed. If we get there today, we might find footprints and see where that guy went."

"Yeah!" David said, glancing up from his artwork. "And if the owner is there, we'll tell him we're on official business."

"What kind of business would that be?" Claire asked. She passed around some bubble gum that she had stored all winter in a knot-hole of the pine tree. The gum was stale, but it tasted good just the same.

David crossed his arms, chewing and thinking. His T-shirt was inside out and wrinkled from having been under his bed for days. "Hmm . . . I know! We can deliver some junk of our own."

"I like the way you think," said Jeff. "We'll surprise Mom by cleaning out the garage." Unlike his younger brother, Jeff enjoyed being organized. He tried to keep his clothes from ending up on their bedroom floor, so as a result his T-shirt today was only slightly rumpled.

Claire was eager to begin their mission. "Then what're we waiting for!" she cried.

Without further discussion, they gathered their backpacks and hurried through the woods to their canoe. Dogs aboard and life preservers on, the cousins paddled across the lake.

The Bridger garage was packed. There were tools, bicycles, camping and ski gear, lawn chairs, fishing poles, and a contraption the children called their "caboose." It was a home-made wagon that attached to the back of Jeff's bike and allowed them to haul things.

"Here're some old blankets," Claire said, carrying an armload from a shelf.

"I'll get these clay pots!" said David. "Who wants to plant flowers, anyway?"

"This rabbit cage is no good anymore," Jeff announced.

"Neither is this stool."

"Or this crate."

Soon the caboose was full. The brothers volunteered to make lunch before setting out for town.

"I'll get my bike. Be right back," Claire said. With Yum-Yum, she ran across the creek to her cabin, leaping from rock to rock. She changed into a purple windbreaker and red sneakers, then dressed her poodle in a matching outfit — a tiny purple sweater with a red collar.

Claire returned by the footbridge that connected the families' yards. She liked the *thumpity-thump* of her wheels on the wood, and the ringing of Yum-Yum's bell as the poodle sat in the basket on her handlebars.

But as she rode up to the Bridger cabin, she was startled by the shriek of a smoke alarm. Tessie and Rascal were barking and barking. There was a terrible odor of burning plastic. Claire grabbed Yum-Yum, dropped her bike on the porch, and burst into the kitchen.

Jeff was opening windows and David was fanning the smoke alarm with a paper plate so it would stop beeping.

"*Pee-ew*, it stinks in here! What happened?" she cried. She grabbed a newspaper and joined them in trying to clear the smoke.

"David was heating spaghetti in the microwave," Jeff reported. "In an old margarine tub."

"You're not supposed to use those things."

"I know, I know!" David said. "I forgot. Then I pushed the wrong buttons."

"He meant to heat it for two minutes," Jeff said.

"But I added an extra zero by accident," David explained.

Claire's eyes grew wide. "You mean *twenty* minutes? You could've burned the house down."

"I figured it out when the smoke alarm went crazy, but it's still a big mess."

The cousins looked in the microwave. The spaghetti was black. The margarine tub had melted over the turntable and spattered up the sides. They tried washing it with a sponge, but the plastic wouldn't come off. They squirted it with dish soap, then set the timer for one minute, but the motor was silent.

"It's busted," said David. "Now what, Jeff?"

"I don't know. It's the second one we've wrecked. Mom is *not* going to be happy. I bet she'll ground us again."

"But vacation just started!" David cried. "We'll be stuck inside for days."

Claire was trying to peel off the skate-board decals the brothers had pasted to the sides of the microwave a few years ago. "These things won't budge," she reminded them. "Maybe we should just take it to the junkyard and buy a new one for Aunt Daisy. We can use the money that we've been hiding out on Lost Island."

The boys thought a moment.

"Okay," Jeff said, taking charge. "Let's load the caboose. I'll make us peanut butter sandwiches. Then we better get going. Rascal can stay here to keep old Tessie company."

3

KIDS KEEP OUT!!

The shortcut to town went through the woods. The lake was a blue flash on their left as the cousins rode over the bumpy dirt trail. Claire led the way with Yum-Yum in her basket, white ears flapping and collar jingling. The caboose bounced behind Jeff's bike with a loud rattle.

"Turn up here," David shouted. A narrow path branched off through a grove of aspen. It was littered with twigs and exposed tree roots, making the ride bumpier. Though the afternoon was sunny, it was cold in the deep shade of the forest. The children pedaled fast to keep warm.

Soon they saw the barbed-wire fence. They skidded to a stop. Signs painted in huge red letters said: POISON and KIDS KEEP OUT!!

The junkyard was a fabulous mess of rusty tools, bicycles, lawn mowers, furniture, and huge tractor tires. In the bed of an old pickup truck there was a couch and a coffee table.

"Maybe the owner lives in that truck," said David. "Should we call to him?"

"Let's find the entrance first," Jeff replied.

The children walked their bikes around the edge of the junkyard until they reached a dirt road. Danger signs were posted on trees and

fence posts, but the gate was open. They stared inside.

"I like this place!" said David. "Let's go in. I bet these signs are just a fake-out."

Jeff regarded their caboose. "How about we unload this stuff first, then find where that guy crawled under the fence? Let's see where he went."

"I'm on it!" Claire cried. She carried the flowerpots to the gate and stood there for a moment to see what would happen. One step inside, then two steps.

"You there!" came a man's gruff voice.

Jeff and David stopped mid-track, the bulky microwave in their arms.

"Hello?" Jeff said.

"Can't you kids read?" the voice shouted.

"It's dangerous in here. Spilled chemicals are everywhere."

"We're on official business, sir," David called. "Just dropping stuff off."

"I'll give you till the count of three to get outta here," the man yelled. "One!"

The brothers set the microwave inside the gate.

"Two!"

Claire deposited the blankets and rabbit cage. David rolled in the stool as Jeff tossed the crate.

"Three!"

The cousins jumped on their bikes and raced along the forested trail for town.

*   *   *

Cabin Creek Animal Hospital had a patio with a picnic table. The boys' mother, Dr. Daisy Bridger, was there eating lunch when the children parked their bikes under a nearby tree.

"How nice to see you kids," she called, waving them over. She had long blond hair braided down her back and the same blue eyes as David. She was wearing jeans and a fleece vest.

"Hi, Aunt Daisy," said Claire. She scooted onto the bench to hug her aunt. "We're sure glad to see you."

"Is everything all right?" Dr. Bridger asked.

The three looked at one another. They had agreed not to tell about their morning in the lookout tower — not yet, anyway.

Finally, Jeff spoke up. "Mom, we had a little problem when we were heating spaghetti in the microwave."

"Oh?"

"Yeah," said David. "Now nothing happens when we push the buttons. Actually, the thing is busted."

Dr. Bridger patted the bench, inviting her sons to sit. "Then I've got some good news. One of my clients gave me his business card this morning. He repairs all sorts of kitchen items. Since we can't afford to buy another microwave, we'll take ours to him. It's better to try to fix things that are broken, that's what your dad always said."

The boys' father, a forest ranger, had died in an avalanche the previous winter. Jeff and David were quiet, remembering him. Then they glanced at Claire. Without saying so, the cousins knew they must hurry back to the junkyard.

"We should get going," said Jeff.

Dr. Bridger was gathering her lunch wrappers. "Same here," she said. "But before you leave, come inside for a few minutes. Something peculiar happened this morning. I'll show you."

4

A New Shortcut

The animal hospital was noisy with barking dogs and Ringo the parrot.

"Hello? Hello?" the bird said from his cage by the door.

"Hi, Ringo," the cousins called as they walked through the reception area. The parrot was bigger than Yum-Yum, who barked and yipped at him from the safety of Claire's arms.

"What? What?" the parrot squawked in return.

"This way, kids," said Dr. Bridger. She was used to the parrot arguing with people. She grabbed her white coat from a hook and put it on while leading them to a back room.

A cardboard box sat on a table. Inside were three baby raccoons, curled together like kittens. Hot water bottles wrapped in towels were keeping them warm.

"Oh, they're so cute," Claire exclaimed.

Dr. Bridger smiled. "These little fellas were on the back step this morning when I came to work. Someone put them in a doll carriage, of all things, and it's odd that the person didn't leave a note. People always tell me where they find lost animals. This helps me know how to

treat them and where to release them back into the wild. Does this belong to any of your friends, Claire?" She pointed to a pink baby buggy in the corner.

"I don't think so, Aunt Daisy. Would my friends be in trouble?"

"No, dear. It's just that I worry about children handling wildlife because of rabies and other diseases. I want kids to know they should call a ranger for help."

"How old are these guys?" asked David.

"Probably three or four weeks old, since they're beginning to open their eyes. Too young to survive on their own." She touched her stethoscope to the furry chests and listened to their hearts.

"I wonder where their mother is," said Jeff.

"Good question," Dr. Bridger answered. "A mother raccoon won't abandon her young unless she's been injured or killed. Or if their den has been disturbed, she'll return for her babies, one by one. Maybe someone saw these cubs while their mom was out looking for food, and thought they were orphans."

The cousins exchanged a look of concern. They were remembering the skull and cross-bones sign at the junkyard.

"They look kinda limp," Jeff said. "Have they been . . . poisoned?"

"I'm running some tests," she answered. "Babies can get sick from their mother's milk if she's eaten something toxic. Last month, a friend of mine brought in two wolf pups, but they didn't survive. I just hope there's nothing in the woods making these animals ill. Okay, kids, I need to get back to work." She washed her hands at the sink, then gave each child a hug.

"Oh, by the way," she said. "Our families are having dinner tonight at the café, six o'clock. And when we get home, maybe you three can help me. Since it's spring break, a lot of folks have left town and have boarded their pets here. I need to gather some extra blankets and cages I've been saving in the garage, for just this sort of thing."

Behind the animal hospital, the forest was thick with pine and oak trees.

"We have to hurry," Claire urged the boys. "Aunt Daisy needs those things we dumped."

Jeff took his compass from his backpack.

"Okay, but first we should know where we're going," he said, looking at the sun. "The lake is northwest from here. Let's find a new short-cut, so we can get there quicker."

David opened his notebook and sketched a map of their location. Claire pointed to a clearing in the woods. "Is the junkyard that way?"

Jeff turned the compass as David drew, then again the boys looked at the sun's position in the sky.

"Yes, I think so," the older brother answered. "But if we miss it, at least we'll be going in a straight line and we'll see the lake. The trail to town is there, so we won't be lost."

Thirty minutes later, the cousins saw the shiny glimmer of barbed wire. They got off their bikes and crept toward the gate, but it was closed with a heavy chain and padlock.

"We can't get in!" Claire cried.

They peered through the fence, trying to see where they had left the microwave and other items. Yum-Yum sniffed in circles at the many footprints, then she rolled in the dirt to scratch her back.

"Our stuff is gone!" David said. "We've only been away a couple hours and already someone swiped everything."

"Maybe it was the man who yelled at us," said Claire.

Jeff tried to be logical. "Well, it *is* his junkyard," he said. "And we did dump our stuff here."

"But Aunt Daisy needs those blankets and rabbit cage," Claire insisted. "I feel so lame. We should've asked before we loaded up our caboose."

Jeff and David walked along the fence, jumping to look over crates, and ducking to look under a tractor, then under a rusted car. There was no other entrance. They couldn't find where the man had crawled out.

Jeff looked at his watch. "It's almost four-thirty. If we get to the café before dinner, we can have a meeting in our special booth. Maybe we'll think of something. Want to, guys?"

"It's the best we can do right now," said Claire. She brushed the dirt from Yum-Yum's sweater, then set her in the basket for their ride through the woods.

5

A Stern Warning

The cousins coasted down a dirt road to Main Street, then pedaled around the corner to the Western Café. They went inside. Yum-Yum stayed in her basket to guard the bikes.

Families on vacation filled all the tables except a corner booth. It looked out onto the sidewalk and was the cousins' favorite meeting place in town.

Though Claire was the youngest, she liked to start their discussions.

"David, could you please take notes again?" she asked. "I like how your drawings help us keep track of the clues."

"Sure thing, boss," he said.

An older waitress brought a plate of carrots and celery sticks. Her name tag read PHYLLIS. "From your folks," the woman said, nodding to the couple behind the grill.

Claire waved to her parents, Aunt Lilly and Uncle Wyatt. They owned the café and were always glad to see the children. Aunt Lilly and Dr. Bridger were sisters.

"Thank you, Miss Phyllis," the cousins said. They waited until she left.

"Now," said Claire, in a soft voice, "we saw a guy in the junkyard this morning. He threw a suitcase of stuff over the fence and crawled under it. Then baby raccoons showed up in a toy buggy, but the only girls I know with dolls are away this week."

"Got it." David drew the carriage with three little raccoons and, for fun, gave them cowboy hats and smiley faces. Then, sketching the microwave, he said, "Mom's not going to be happy — "

"Hello, my favorite scallywags," said an elderly man who had just come into the café. He had a white beard and fluffy white hair, and was dressed for dinner in a red plaid shirt. He was a special friend of the Bridger and Posey families and often shared meals with them. "I'm early, mind if I join you?"

"Have a seat!" the children said, scooting over to make room. Gus Penny was the man's real name, but they called him Mr. Wellback because of the way he began his stories. He always said, "Well, back when I was a boy . . ."

David showed Mr. Wellback his drawings while Jeff and Claire described the unusual events of the day.

"My, my," he said, furrowing his bushy white eyebrows, "you've gotten yourselves into a pickle this time, that's for ding-dong sure. What's your next move?"

"If we can't get our things back from the junkyard, I bet Mom will ground us for the week," Jeff said. "We'll need after-school jobs to buy a new microwave and other stuff."

A busboy brought a pitcher of ice water with cups. Then he began setting the table with napkins and silverware.

"Thank you, son," Mr. Wellback said to the teenager, taking a drink. "Where were we? Oh, yes. Microwaves. On that subject, I've been thinking I could use one. Phyllis here said baked potatoes take eight minutes, and you can heat leftovers, though I've never minded a pan of cold beans for supper. It's like camping."

The cousins grinned. Their friend lived up a twisty road in a rustic log cabin. He cooked on a potbellied stove, refused to own a TV, and only just had a telephone installed the month before. He chopped his own firewood and spent long hours on his porch with his hound dogs, admiring his view of the lake. Thinking of Mr. Wellback with a microwave was just plain funny.

"But back to your dilemma," he said. "That

junkyard is no place for kids, even though the new owner is cleaning things up. A taste of antifreeze from an old engine can be deadly to animals. And if you were to cut yourselves on a rusty something-or-other, you could get lockjaw."

"What's that?" David asked.

"Well, back when I was ten years old, one of my buddies stepped on a rusty nail and got blood poisoning. After a few days, his jaws locked up and he couldn't open his mouth to breathe. Suffocated to death. Terrible. Nowadays, folks can get a tetanus shot, but the vaccines don't last forever."

"*Lockjaw*," the cousins whispered. It was a terrifying idea.

"Are you whippersnappers listening to me?"

They nodded, eyes wide. *Lockjaw.* They tried to imagine the boy from long ago. They were also hoping a mother raccoon hadn't tasted any antifreeze.

"Good," said Mr. Wellback. "Now, you stay away from that place."

6

The Predicament

Mr. Wellback sat quietly in the booth while his young friends described their predicament to their parents. He gave a sympathetic look, as if he remembered being young himself and getting into trouble.

Jeff and David's mom sprinkled pepper onto her salad, then added dressing. "Your hearts were in the right place," she said to the children, "but next time, instead of dumping things at a junkyard where they'll rot and rust, let's first try to repair them. Or we can donate somewhere."

"Like donate to people in need?" David asked.

"That's the idea," said Uncle Wyatt. He leaned over to give his nephews a fatherly rub on their shoulders.

Aunt Lilly was passing a platter of ham and potatoes. Her red hair was brushed back like Claire's, her green eyes thoughtful. "Hmm," she said. "I think we can find extra chores here during spring break. It'll help you kids earn money toward a new microwave."

"And I, too, could use your help," said Dr. Bridger. "Along with extra blankets and a rabbit cage, I need a shelf for the waiting room, you know, for magazines and pamphlets. I'm doing some remodeling. Instead of buying new things, you can check the want ads and yard sales for me. Thrift stores are great, too."

"Here you go, folks," said Phyllis. She set freshly baked rolls on the table with butter and jam.

Mr. Wellback offered the rolls to the cousins. They were sitting with their hands in their laps, sober from their confession. "It's all right, children," he said. "Let's have our supper now. Tomorrow is a brand-new day."

The next morning after breakfast, the threesome rode through the woods for town. This time they ignored the trail to the junkyard. They parked their bikes at the library and checked the bulletin board. Then they went to the community center, hardware store, and market to read the want ads. But so far, no one was selling a used microwave or any of the other things Dr. Bridger needed.

At the bakery, the kids bought a small sack of cookies to share while they peeked in the window of a secondhand store. It was closed, so they walked around the corner to a quiet neighborhood. At one of the cottages, they stopped to admire a bright yellow bicycle behind a picket fence. It had high, curved handlebars with tassels and a low-rider seat.

"Look, Sophie left her bike out front," said Jeff. "Too bad she's gone all week."

"Yeah, she loves mysteries and could be helping us," Claire said. Their friend, Sophie Garcia, was visiting her grandparents in Montana.

David opened the little gate and walked over to the bike. He squeezed the rubber horn.

A-oooga . . . a-oooga!

"Cool!" the boys cried.

"Bet we could do some jumps on this baby." David sat on the cushioned seat and bounced up and down. "Think Sophie would mind if we took 'er for a spin?"

"Guys —" Claire hesitated.

"Sophie won't mind at all," Jeff declared. "Remember how she let me use her snowboard all winter, and I let her use my helmet? She likes it when we share our stuff. You first, David."

Claire watched as the brothers took turns skidding around the driveway and up the road. *A-oooga . . . a-oooga!*

"Come on, Claire, you try!" Jeff screeched to a stop in a spray of dirt. "It's almost lunchtime. Let's head for the café. David and I'll run beside you like we're in a relay race or something. We can bring the bike back after we eat."

"What're you kids doing?" called a lady from her porch at the cottage next door. It was Mrs. O'Neal, their former kindergarten teacher. She was in the odd circumstance of holding a toaster with black smoke puffing out of it. The cord dangled by her slippered feet. "I said, what are you doing with my neighbor's bike?"

"Hi, Mrs. O'Neal," they greeted her, waving.

"Sophie's our friend, so we share things," David said. His clothes were dusty from his joyride, his blond hair unruly.

"Did your toaster catch on fire?" Claire asked.

"Indeed it did," the woman replied. "It happens about once a week, so I bring it out here to cool off. Crumbs get stuck inside and burn. It's a stinking mess and hard to clean. Are you sure it's okay for you to fool around with that bike?"

"Positive," said Jeff.

"All right, then. Make sure you return it in the same condition in which you found it."

"Yes, ma'am! Have a nice day, Mrs. O'Neal."

The Western Café was busy with tourists, so the children sat at the counter. While waiting for their hamburgers, they giggled about Mrs. O'Neal.

"It's the first time we've seen a teacher on her porch holding a toaster." Jeff laughed.

"Especially one that was smoking!" David laughed even harder.

"And she was wearing slippers!" Claire threw her head back with a loud *HAW!* But just then she noticed her father coming into the dining area.

"Excuse me, folks," Uncle Wyatt announced. "Did anyone leave a yellow bicycle in the alley here? I'm terribly sorry, but a vegetable truck just ran over it."

7

A Dreadful Mistake

Sophie's pretty yellow bike was mangled. The *a-oooga* horn had popped open and the handlebars were flattened.

Uncle Wyatt looked out from under the brim of his cowboy hat. "What on earth were you kids thinking?"

The cousins stared at the ground.

"You have your own bicycles, yet you borrow a friend's without asking? Then you leave it in the path of delivery trucks while enjoying your lunch?"

"We're sorry," each child said in a small voice.

"It's Sophie you'll need to apologize to. Now what are you going to do to repair this?"

The brothers looked up and shrugged. Claire, too.

Uncle Wyatt removed his hat and tapped the dust out of it against his knee. "Tell you what," he said, shaking his head. "I'll bring it home in the Jeep, then we can go through the sheds and garage for spare parts. That is, unless you kids hauled everything to the junkyard already."

"No, Daddy," said Claire. "We didn't take anything from our place."

"Okay. In the meantime, Aunt Lilly has

potatoes in the kitchen for you three to wash and peel."

Miss Phyllis went home early, so the cousins filled water glasses, then helped the busboy clear tables. Finally, Uncle Wyatt said they could leave.

"Good job, kids," he said to them. "Tonight we're all having dinner at your place, boys. Gus is coming, too. See you then."

The children left the café by its front door. For the moment, they were too discouraged to even go look at the yellow bike. They headed for the library. Mrs. O'Neal happened to be coming down the steps with a book bag over her shoulder.

"There you are!" she said. "I was thinking about having a chat with your parents."

"Is anything wrong?" Claire asked.

"Anything wrong? Someone has taken my toaster! Right off my front porch, in broad daylight. Do you youngsters know anything about this?"

The cousins looked at one another, mystified.

"Mrs. O'Neal, we would never take anything off your porch," Jeff insisted.

"Is that so?" she said. "Well, you didn't hesitate to take a bike from my neighbor's yard. Then, two hours later, my toaster vanished. Do you see why I might suspect the three of you?"

"Yes, ma'am," said David. "But please believe us. We didn't steal your toaster. We don't even like toast."

The cousins wanted to surprise their parents by having dinner ready for them.

In the Bridger kitchen, Jeff made macaroni and cheese while Claire and David cut vegetables for a salad. Together, they set the table for seven people, swept the floor, and fed the dogs. They turned the oven to 350 degrees. Then they arranged hot dogs in a pan and decorated them with dribbles of ketchup and mustard.

The hot dogs had been baking for fifteen minutes when Mr. Wellback knocked on the door with his hiking stick. His white hair was windblown from his walk.

"Mm, something's cooking," he said. He took a box of graham crackers from his rucksack and set it on the counter. "Here's dessert! I'll get a plate."

Soon the boys' mom came in. "You kids made dinner? What a wonderful surprise. Thank you! My, the table is set and everything. Hello there, Gus."

Next, Aunt Lilly and Uncle Wyatt walked in through the sunroom. Uncle Wyatt hung his hat on the coatrack, then hugged his daughter. Smiling, he shook hands with his nephews. "Very thoughtful of you kids to make dinner. You've sure been busy."

"Daddy," said Claire, "we also found a wheel and some handlebars in our shed. Maybe after the dishes are done, we can start fixing Sophie's bike?"

"Good idea."

"I'll put it in the driveway," Jeff volunteered. "Come on, David."

A few minutes later, the brothers returned to the kitchen. "Uncle Wyatt? Where'd you put the yellow bike?"

"What do you mean?" their uncle asked.

"It's not in the Jeep," David said.

Uncle Wyatt gave the cousins a quizzical look. "Of course not. This afternoon when I came out of the café, the bike was gone. I assumed you kids had carted it home in your caboose."

They looked at him with wide eyes. Their shoulders sagged.

"So you *didn't* bring it home?" Uncle Wyatt asked them.

They shook their heads no.

Sophie's bike had disappeared.

8

Fort Grizzly Paw

The next morning was cool and damp from the night's rain. The cousins met on the dock in front of their cabins in warm sweatshirts. Their backpacks were loaded with their usual supplies — walkie-talkies, candy, snacks, and dog biscuits. Canoeing was so familiar to them that in minutes they had snapped on their life vests, loaded the dogs, and were paddling to Lost Island.

Their mission today was serious.

"Spring break just started," Jeff reminded them, "but we keep getting in trouble. We have to figure things out before we get thrown in the slammer."

When they arrived in the protected cove, they pulled their craft up on the beach so it wouldn't float away with the tide. A wooded trail led them to Fort Grizzly Paw, which was in a clearing. There was the good smell of pine needles baking in the sun. The children marched around all sides of the log cabin before going inside, inspecting the dirt for human footprints.

"No one's been here!" Claire cried. "Let's have lunch and start the meeting!" She opened the picket gate they had installed in the broken wall. The dogs followed her in, then curled up together on the old sleeping bag.

"I'll get the drinks," said Jeff. He poured water from his canteen into tin cups. Claire arranged a plate of potato chips and fig bars on the table as David opened his sketchbook. With a black marker, he drew the disaster of yesterday: Sophie's scrunched-up bicycle. Then he read their list of troubles.

"Sophie's bike is our fault," he said, "and so is Mom's stuff. But we don't know what happened to Mrs. O'Neal's toaster. Or why that guy sneaked out of the junkyard with a suitcase."

"And we don't know if a kid or a grown-up put those raccoons in a doll carriage," said Claire. She tapped her finger on David's drawing. "But this is our worst problem. I won't blame Sophie one bit if she dumps us. Her parents probably won't let us hang out anymore."

Jeff closed his eyes, thinking. "We can give her *my* bike, and tell her we made a really stupid mistake."

"A really *big*, stupid mistake," David added.

"Okay, let's get busy." Claire went to the pine tree that was growing out of the floor. She reached into all the knotholes where she had hidden small treasures, such as her purple shoelaces and a glow-in-the-dark bracelet. When she returned to their table, she poured out a handful of coins and dollar bills.

"Eight bucks exactly," she said.

Jeff was at the fireplace, removing a stone above the mantel. Out came a tuna can wrapped in foil. "Five bucks and twenty-two cents," he said, after counting.

David started digging in a corner. He pulled out a dirty gym sock full of nickels, pennies, and dimes. It clunked onto the table like a heavy rock. He said, "The last time I looked, there was at least ten dollars here."

The cousins put their savings in their backpacks and whistled for the dogs.

After canoeing across the lake, they left their pets in the Bridger cabin and rode to town. It was late afternoon when they reached Benny & June's Used Stuff. June, a plump yellow cat, was stretched out in the sunny window. She regarded the children with drowsy green eyes.

When they went over to pet her, her purring grew loud, like a small motor.

The shop smelled like fresh paint. Its floor and shelves displayed a fascinating clutter of secondhand toys and books, furniture, saddles, radios, luggage, and camping gear.

"Can I help you, kids?" asked Benny, a young man on a stepladder. He was painting a wall light blue with purple trim. His sweater was ragged and spattered with paint.

"Do you have a little bookshelf?" Jeff asked. "Our mom needs one for the animal clinic, and we're also looking for a microwave."

Benny set his paintbrush in a can of water, then checked in a back room. "Sorry," he said, "maybe tomorrow. I get new stuff every day."

Claire took a toaster from the shelf. "Excuse me, sir. How much is this?"

Benny put on a pair of glasses to inspect it. "Mm. Give me two bucks and we'll call it even."

"Thanks!" Claire dug in her pocket and paid in quarters. "Guys, before we head back home, let's surprise Mrs. O'Neal."

They parked their bikes in front of the teacher's cottage, happy to be doing a good deed.

"I'm tired of getting in trouble," said Jeff. "This was a great idea, Claire."

"Definitely," David agreed.

When Mrs. O'Neal opened the door, they shouted, "Surprise!"

"My word," the woman said. "I don't know

what to say except . . . thank you. But I can't accept your gift. This certainly is a day of surprises. Come in for a moment, won't you?"

Mrs. O'Neal led the children into her kitchen. On the counter was a toaster. It was identical to the one she had put on her porch the day before, except this one was shiny with a red bow on top. Its cord was folded as if she had just taken it out of its box.

"Oh, you bought a new one," said Claire. She tried not to sound disappointed.

"No, dear. This is mine. It has the same dent on the side, from when I dropped it last Christmas. Do you kids know anything about this? You're the only ones I told about it being hard to clean."

"We didn't tell anyone, either," David replied.

"Then this is a real puzzle," she said. "See, when I went out to get the newspaper this morning, I was flabbergasted to find my toaster. Someone had returned it all spiffed up, with a ribbon and a bow. Don't get me wrong, I'm grateful, but it's strange. Very strange. As if someone is spying on us."

9

Another Surprise

Claire put the two-dollar toaster in her basket, then walked her bike beside Jeff and David. They didn't feel like riding. They were mystified about what had happened on Mrs. O'Neal's porch.

"Things sure are weird around here," Jeff said, and David and Claire agreed.

When they turned the corner to Oak Street, they saw a man in overalls working under a red pickup truck. Only his boots stuck out from under the engine. A bottle of Spray-and-Clean sat by his feet.

"Hello, kids!" a voice called. To their surprise, a woman slid out from under the truck on a rolling board. She sat up in the driveway and opened a large toolbox. Taking out a wrench, she said, "Too tired to ride today?"

"Miss Phyllis? What're you doing here?"

"A girl can change the oil on her truck, can't she?" The woman laughed. "I have lots to do on my day off. Next, I'm painting my front door. Say, what's with the toaster?"

"Oh, this?" Claire sighed. "Long story. We won't bore you."

"Suit yourself."

The cousins got on their bikes and hurried through town to the lake. They didn't talk until they were in the woods where no one could hear them.

"Miss Phyllis is a fix-it lady!" Jeff cried. "And she wears overalls and boots, just like the guy in the junkyard."

Claire said, "Hey, what if she heard us at the café yesterday, talking about Mrs. O'Neal's toaster? Maybe she sneaked over to pick it up. She left before we finished our burgers, remember?"

"Yeah!" David exclaimed. "Then she polished it with Spray-and-Clean, added ribbon and a bow, then took it back early this morning."

"But why would she go to all that trouble?" Claire asked.

Jeff brushed the hair out of his eyes to

look back through the trees. "Maybe Miss Phyllis isn't the only one who wanted to do a good deed."

The next day before lunch, the cousins visited the animal hospital. Dr. Bridger had just finished feeding the baby raccoons when they entered the room. She was at the sink filling plastic juice bottles with hot water, and handed one to each child with a roll of duct tape.

"Tape these to the insides of the box," she instructed, "so the bottles won't roll onto the cubs and hurt them. This is another way to keep them warm, unlike heating lamps, which can get too hot."

"Are they going to live?" David asked.

"They're in good shape now," Dr. Bridger replied. "They'll do fine."

The children stroked the babies with a finger. Each tiny head was soft, like a small peach. Markings around the eyes made the raccoons look like they were wearing black masks.

"I wish we could keep them for pets," Jeff said.

"Me, too," said David.

"Same here!" Claire agreed. "But they're not mellow like Benny's cat. They would climb into the kitchen cupboards and wreck things, right, Aunt Daisy?"

Dr. Bridger laughed. "That's true. By the time these cubs are old enough for us to return them to the woods, they'll be getting into everything." Her braid swung over her shoulder as she bent down to open a cupboard. She took out an armful of brochures on heartworm medicine and other veterinary helps.

"Now I can finally put these out where folks can read them. I'm most grateful to you children."

The cousins looked at one another.

"What're you talking about, Mom?" Jeff asked.

Again she laughed. "You kids didn't waste any time. When I was out in the patio eating lunch, Ringo sounded the alert. He made such a racket I went inside, but I guess you already had left by the back door. So sweet of you to surprise me."

"Mom —" David began.

"Here, you can help." She handed each child a stack of pamphlets and led them into the waiting room.

Under the window was a small bookshelf. It was blue with green trim and smelled of fresh paint.

10

Someone Is Watching

Ringo waddled back and forth in his cage. "Hello? What? What?" he kept squawking. Claire gave him a peanut from the jar on the counter so he would be quiet. She and the boys were trying to examine the bookshelf.

"It's the same blue paint that Benny was using on his wall," Jeff said. "And he knew Mom needed a shelf because we told him so."

"Another thing," said Claire. "Remember how we wondered if that guy snagged his clothes on the barbed wire?"

"Yeah?"

"Well, I noticed some holes in Benny's sleeve when I paid him my two dollars."

David said, "Maybe he goes to the junkyard. He told us he gets new stuff every day."

Just then, Dr. Bridger returned from her office with a paper sack. "On your way home, kids, would you please take this to Gus? His dogs need toothpaste and vitamins."

"I'll put 'em in my basket," Claire offered. "Aunt Daisy, do you like your new shelf?"

"Yes," she answered. "I'm curious, though, why someone is sneaking around, even if it is a good deed."

The children then told Dr. Bridger she wasn't the only one in town with a mysterious delivery.

"Mrs. O'Neal, too?" she said. "I wonder if this person also brought in the orphaned raccoons."

"Should we call the police?" Jeff asked.

Dr. Bridger put her hands in the pockets of her lab coat. She had the same thoughtful expression as her sons. "I don't think we need to report this. No laws have been broken."

"And besides," said Claire, feeding the parrot another nut, "Ringo is our only witness."

"Some witness," said David. "He talks, but he doesn't say anything."

*　　　*　　　*

When the cousins reached the winding road that led to Mr. Wellback's place, they stopped at the bottom of the hill. They hid their bikes in the trees. It was easier to hike up with their backpacks, instead of ride. Even so, they were out of breath when they reached the crest and saw his cabin. Its log roof and log walls were weathered to a pale gray. His view of the lake was beautiful.

Several hunting dogs loped from their napping spots in the shade, howling and barking to announce the visitors. Mr. Wellback came onto his porch.

"Come in!" He waved to the children. "You lollygaggers are just in time for lunch." He looked cheerful in his plaid shirt, blue jeans, and spanking-white sneakers.

"Mm, smells good," the kids said, stepping into the small cabin.

Three surprises awaited them.

The first was a microwave oven. It was perched on a kitchen stool because there was only enough space on the counter for Mr. Wellback's radio. He clicked open the glass door to show what he had been cooking.

"Phyllis was right," he said. "Eight minutes for a potato. I've also made some popcorn and scrambled eggs. You scallywags are too good to me. I thank you kindly."

That was their second surprise: He thought this was a gift from them.

Then, their third surprise: Mr. Wellback's new microwave was covered with skateboard decals.

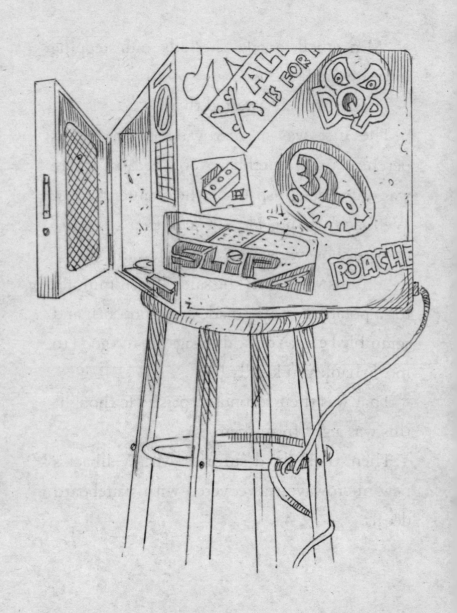

"Hey!" Jeff cried. "This is the one we left at the junkyard! Sir, how did you find this?"

"What do you mean, sonny?" When he saw the children's confused faces he said, "So you rascals didn't have this delivered up here? You're the only ones I've told about wanting one of these things."

They were shaking their heads no.

Mr. Wellback gazed out his window, where a patch of blue lake could be seen through the trees. "Now, let me think a moment. Oh, yes. After breakfast, I heard the dogs outside making a big ruckus. I was engrossed in my crossword puzzle, so it took a minute to get out of my chair and onto the porch. Could hardly believe it, but this microwave was right there. I noticed dust going down the road, and a red car, but couldn't see who was driving."

"What kind of car?" asked Jeff.

"Mm, the engine coughed and popped. But now that I think on it, it reminded me of an old bumpity pickup I used to have."

"Do you mean a red pickup truck?" Claire asked.

The elderly man nodded. "If I had to guess I'd say, yessir, a red pickup truck."

11

More Questions

Before the cousins hiked back down the hill, Mr. Wellback served them his new favorite lunch: baked potatoes topped with applesauce and nutmeg.

"I'll return this microwave to your mother," he told the boys.

"We think you should keep it, sir," said David. When he and Jeff had seen how much fun Mr. Wellback was having pushing all the buttons and cooking things, they had whispered to each other.

"We're going to ask Mom," said Jeff, "but knowing her, she'll be really glad you can use this. And we'll get her another one. Without skateboard stickers."

The cousins sat in a window seat eating their potatoes. Mr. Wellback brought them each a glass of water. "You scoundrels are good at solving mysteries," he said. "What are your clues so far?"

David reached for the backpack at his feet and took out his sketch pad. As he flipped through his drawings, he noticed one of the pages was missing.

"My map!" he said. "It's gone. I must've ripped it out by accident. It had our shortcut to town and the road up here to your cabin —

hey, wait a minute! Maybe someone found it and that's how they drove up here."

Claire leaned over to look at the torn paper. "David, when did you draw this map?"

"At the café, I think. Yeah! That's where we were."

"Okay," said Jeff, "let's figure this out. Who was at the café when we were talking about a microwave?"

"The busboy," David replied. "Miss Phyllis. Tourists at the next table."

"What other oddities have happened?" Mr. Wellback asked the children.

"First, the raccoon babies appeared," Claire said, "then Mrs. O'Neal's toaster was taken, then Sophie's bike went missing. Now Aunt Daisy's bookshelf."

The children studied David's drawings.

"Miss Phyllis has a red pickup truck," Jeff said. "And we saw her wearing overalls and boots like the guy sneaking out of the junkyard."

Claire said, "Maybe she and Benny are working together. I noticed a suitcase in his shop yesterday, plus his sweater was ripped."

"Hold it, guys," said Jeff. "Since someone is doing all this in secret, maybe they want to keep it that way. What do you think, sir?"

Their friend went to the microwave to warm up his potato. "Well, back when I was a boy, we were taught to do good without tooting our own horns."

"Tooting a horn?"

"It means not bragging," he answered.

"But swiping Sophie's bike from the alley wasn't a good deed," David said.

"Neither was riding it away from her house, young man."

At the bottom of Mr. Wellback's hill, the cousins dragged their bikes out from the trees. They looked at the trail. Westward led to their cabins on the far shore. Eastward went to town. And to the junkyard.

Jeff looked at his watch. "It's only one-thirty. We have all afternoon."

"But Mr. Wellback told us it's dangerous," Claire said. "What about the poison signs, and getting lockjaw? And what if the owner is there yelling —"

"We'll be extra super careful," David reassured her. "We have all our gear. Flashlights and whistles, your first-aid kit. And we just had lunch so we won't starve if we get locked in. Besides, we can call Uncle Wyatt on our walkie-talkies."

"Should we have a plan first?" she asked.

Jeff got on his bike and pointed it east. "I'm thinking of one right now."

"So we're sneaking into the junkyard?" Claire said, also getting on her bike.

David spun his back wheel with a little jump. "Yeah!" he yelled. "We're sneaking in!"

⑫
An Unlikely Friend

The junkyard gate was locked. After hiding their bikes, the cousins crept along the fence, looking for a way to crawl inside. Their voices were quiet.

"Up there, look," said Jeff. He pointed to a hole under the fence where the wire had been pulled up. The space underneath was just big enough for him to wiggle through. "Follow me, guys. You'll fit easy. It's okay."

After they wormed their way in, their knees and elbows were caked with mud. They wandered among stacks of tires, then through a maze of boat engines that smelled like gasoline. From a pile of rags came the buzzing of flies and a stench of dead fish.

Claire grabbed Jeff's arm. "This place gives me the creeps! Do you have a plan yet?"

"I'm still thinking," he said.

"Me, too," said David.

"Well, I think we should leave right now," she whispered. She brushed a fly off her cheek, then squinted to see through an old jungle gym.

"Hey! What's that over there?" Claire pointed to a tangle of bicycles. One of them was yellow. Its front tire and handlebars were missing. "It's Sophie's!"

The children rushed forward. "That's for ding-dong sure!" David cried, imitating Mr. Wellback. "But how'd it get here?"

Jeff clapped his brother on the shoulder. "Who knows? But let's get this baby home and fix 'er up before vacation is over."

"And how are we going to do that?" asked Claire. "It won't go under the fence, and if we throw it over, we'll wreck it even worse —"

"What are you kids doing here?" yelled a familiar voice.

The cousins whirled around to see a man in a tweed coat with a silk scarf around his neck. He was wearing nice pants and shoes, and was smoking a pipe. He looked like a professor.

"I asked you a question," he said, pointing the stem of his pipe at them.

"Uh, we're investigating a mystery," Claire blurted out. "And we found our friend's bike. We need to get it home."

The man sighed with irritation. "I put up all sorts of signs and I lock the gate, but still people get in."

"Excuse me, sir," said David. "Do you live here in an old car with pet tarantulas?"

The man bit down on his pipe, trying not to laugh. "Goodness, where do these stories come from? My wife and I live in an apartment at the Blue Mountain Lodge. She works in the gift shop and I'm the new owner of this place. Signed the final papers last week. Friends are helping me clean it up so we can turn it into a swap meet, you know, where folks trade for items they need. I'll charge one dollar to drop things off, and one dollar to take some-thing away."

"But you don't look like a junk man," Claire said, appreciating the man's stylish clothes.

"Well, I am, young lady. Junk is my busi-ness, Fairmont is my name. It happens that I'm on my way to a meeting with the environmen-tal board with my list of dangerous items. They'll help me remove the harmful liquids and so forth." He patted his shirt pocket, where there was a tiny notebook and pen.

"Mr. Fairmont," said Jeff, "we're curious how our friend's bike got here."

The man puffed his pipe, then blew a fabu-lous smoke ring. It resembled a sugar donut, drifting up and up. "I've been driving through the alleys of town to pick up items that people put out for me. The other afternoon, I saw the yellow bike behind the café and added it to my truck."

When he said "truck," the children gave one another a knowing glance.

"Does it happen to be a red pickup?" David asked.

"So many questions! No, it's dark green. Will there be anything else before I shoo you inquisitive children out of here?"

Jeff spoke first.

"Have you seen a mother raccoon in here with any babies?" he asked. "They might be sick on antifreeze or something like that."

The man glanced away. A worried look came to his eyes. "I feel very bad about what happened here. I did find a litter of five. Sadly, the mother and two of her young were dead. I wrapped three cubs in my sweater and hurried to the animal hospital, but it wasn't open yet. I waited until the veterinarian drove up to make sure they'd be safe, then I left. I should have written a note explaining, but I was too ashamed."

"Why?" Jeff inquired.

Again the man looked sad. He shook his head. "I should have had this place inspected before I bought it. I had no idea the former owner left behind so many machines and engines with leaking chemicals."

"Mr. Fairmont, did the doll buggy come from here?" Claire asked.

"Yes. I have a whole section of toys."

"Is it okay if we take our friend's bike?"

"Take it," he said. "In fact, come with me. You can help yourselves to wheels, seats, bells, you name it. Fix it up however you like.

But please don't come in here without my supervision. This will be a very fine junkyard when we're done making it safe, and you'll be able to explore all you want."

"One last question, Mr. Fairmont." Jeff stood tall, glad they had made a friend instead of getting into trouble again. "We need to come back tomorrow with our caboose, to haul the bike and everything home. Is that all right?"

"I'll be here until noon," he replied.

13

An Important Interview

The next morning at the junkyard, Jeff and Claire gathered bicycle parts while David explored. Mr. Fairmont was helping him look for Dr. Bridger's rabbit cage.

The man was dressed in work clothes — jeans, boots, and a baseball cap — as he showed the younger boy around. "Sorry, son, but my wife washed the blankets you left here. She took them to a family in town who needed them. The flowerpots she planted with daisies to cheer up a friend of ours. If something is useful, we try to find a good home for it."

"By any chance, did you see who took our microwave?" David asked. "It's not a big deal, we're just trying to figure some things out."

"I'm only open two hours each morning," said Mr. Fairmont. "It's mostly so my crew and I can clean up and haul away the hazardous items. All sorts of folks have been coming and going, and some even sneak in after I lock up. Sorry I can't help you more."

The caboose rattled and clanked along the trail as the cousins rode into town. They were taking the shortcut they had mapped out a few days earlier. It was time for lunch, but first they stopped at Benny & June's, where the yellow cat was asleep in her favorite window.

"Okay, guys," said Jeff, before going inside. "Since we know Mr. Fairmont picked up Sophie's bike and delivered the raccoons, we can cross those things off our list. What's next?"

David took out his sketchbook and pencil. "I'll start the interview," he said.

Benny was behind the counter, polishing a tray of silver spoons.

"Let me see," he said, when David asked about his freshly painted wall. "I like to barter — that means trade. So I gave my left-over cans of blue and green and purple to a lady. In exchange, she gave me some towels and these spoons."

"Did you happen to get a bookcase after that?" asked Claire. "Remember, we were looking for one?"

"One did come in," he said. "It needed to be sanded and painted, so I traded it to a buddy of mine for a suitcase full of toy cars — see, they're over there in that box? My friend put the shelf in his truck."

Upon hearing the words "truck" and "paint," the cousins smiled at one another.

"It was a red pickup, wasn't it?" Jeff stated.

"And you gave him some paint," said Claire.

"Nope and nope," Benny answered. "My paint was gone by then and the kid's truck was an old beat-up thing, dirty white, like most of the ranchers around here have. You sure ask a lot of questions. Are you with the FBI?"

"We're investigators," Claire said. "There have been some odd happenings in town."

"*Very* odd," David emphasized.

"All right, then," said Benny. "What else do you want to know?"

"Is your friend about sixteen years old?" Jeff asked. He was picturing the busboy who may have overheard their conversations in the café.

"Nope again. He's older. He fixes things that people throw away, then he sells them."

"Thank you, Benny," the children said, petting his cat on their way out.

The cousins parked their caboose in front of the café so they could keep an eye on things. They did not want to lose Sophie's bike again.

Aunt Lilly welcomed them at the door. She and Uncle Wyatt always let the kids eat anything they wanted from the menu.

Phyllis took their order. "Three tuna sandwiches on whole wheat with fries," she repeated to them. "And your usual shakes, right? Chocolate for Jeff, strawberry for Claire, vanilla for David. I remember because the flavors match your hair color. Anything else?"

Claire went first. "Miss Phyllis, remember the other day we saw you changing the oil on your truck, the red one?"

The waitress laughed. "A red truck is the only one I have. What're you getting at?"

"Does anyone else ever drive it?" David asked.

Phyllis put her pencil behind her ear

and gave them a look of curiosity. "Some-times. Why?"

"Order up!" called a voice from the kitchen.

"Excuse me, kids, I need to scoot. Back in a few minutes with your shakes."

14

A New Suspect

"So Miss Phyllis lets other people drive her truck!" Claire exclaimed.

"We definitely need to ask her more questions," David said.

"I'll start this time," said Jeff. He glanced over at the malt machine, where their waitress was scooping ice cream. Soon she carried over three tall milk shakes, all topped with whipped cream and a cherry. She set each glass on a paper doily with a straw and an extra long spoon.

"Thank you," said the cousins. But before they could ask about her truck, she hurried away to the kitchen.

Finally, Phyllis returned to the table, this time balancing plates on her arm. When the cousins didn't start eating their fries as usual, she said, "Okay, out with it. What're you kids up to?"

In a jumble, they related everything that had happened since spring vacation had started.

Phyllis took a bottle of ketchup from her apron pocket and put it on the table. "Oh, dear," she said. "I suppose I'm responsible for part of this confusion. The busboy told me Gus Penny wanted a microwave, then I told my son Matthew. He's living with me to save money for college. Since I can walk to work,

I let Matthew use my pickup for all his odd jobs, though sometimes he borrows our neighbor's."

"Does he like to fix stuff?" David wondered.

"He does. Ever since he was little, he's had a knack for taking things apart and putting them together again. When I heard you kids discussing Mrs. O'Neal's toaster, I mentioned it to him because she was his kindergarten teacher. Matthew really adored her."

"Could we meet your son?" Jeff asked.

The woman looked up at the wall clock. "He's coming by in a few minutes," she said, "to pick up the empty egg cartons and plastic jugs. Wyatt is paying him to take care of all the recycling."

Matthew was taller than his mother and lanky like a basketball player. He wore a university sweatshirt. He greeted the cousins by shaking hands with each one of them, then pulled a chair over to the table.

"I've seen you kids riding bikes around town," he said. "That's a great jalopy you use for hauling stuff. So what's up? Mom says you wanted to ask me something."

They described the toaster. "Wow," Matthew said. "I didn't mean to cause an uproar. Yes, I cleaned it up and replaced the frayed cord. See, when I was in kindergarten, Mrs. O'Neal would always surprise us. Sometimes it would be a cookie at our table when we came in from recess. Or a little box of colored pencils on our birthday. But she never said it was from her. She'd only say that someone cared about us. When I got older I figured it out."

"I like this story," said David.

"As for the bookshelf," Matthew went on, "when my dog was sick, Dr. Bridger took care of him and didn't charge me for the medicine. I've always wanted to do something nice for your mother."

"But how did you know she needed a book-case?" Jeff asked.

"My mother overheard *your* mother in the café. When she told *me*, I went to Benny's shop and found the perfect little shelf. Took it home, sanded it, and used some of my mom's blue and green paint. Then I sneaked it into the clinic while Dr. Bridger was outside eating lunch. That parrot made so much noise, I had to hurry — ha!"

Claire leaned over to whisper to Jeff and David. When the brothers nodded, she said, "Matthew, were you driving an old white pickup that day?"

"Uh . . . let me think. Mom was changing the oil on her truck, so yeah, I borrowed our neighbor's. How did you know?"

"We dabble in detective work," was Jeff's quick reply. "Do you mind if we ask a few more questions?"

A slow smile came to the young man's face. "Of course not."

"Do you ever go to the junkyard when it's closed?"

"Never. But I did get locked in the other day

by accident. I looked all over for Mr. Fairmont, but the only way I could get out was to toss my bag over the fence, then crawl underneath it. Tore my favorite sweatshirt, see?" Matthew showed them the snags down his back.

David flipped open his sketchbook and checked off *Shadowy guy in junkyard*, then did the same with his drawings of the toaster and bookshelf.

"Looks like we're done," Matthew remarked.

"Well, almost," said David. He turned to the page where his map had fallen out.

15

A Personal Matter

"So *you're* the artist!" said Matthew, watching David make a new sketch of the lake and town.

"You've seen this before?" Jeff asked.

"Sort of. I found a map here when I came in for lunch. It showed the road to Gus Penny's cabin. And since my mom said he might like a microwave, one thing led to another. I thought it would be fun to give him a modern gizmo."

Claire scrunched up her nose. "That must mean you cleaned the gross, disgusting spaghetti and the plastic that melted everywhere."

"Sure did," Matthew replied. "Lemon juice, water, and vinegar are great natural cleaners, and they're not chemicals either. The motor had shorted out so I fixed that, too. It was easy."

"But why didn't you take off the skateboard stickers?"

"Listen, I've known Gus all my life, even though I had never been to his place before. He's uncomfortable when people spend money on him, so I left the decals on to prove that it was a used microwave. Any more questions?" Matthew's smile was friendly.

David let out a deep sigh. "Well, this whole

week, we've been curious. How come a person does nice things in secret, like you've been doing? I *want* people to know when we do something good."

"That's because we're always getting in trouble," Jeff laughed, giving his brother a playful nudge.

Matthew squinted in thought. "Mm, I don't know really. Maybe because it makes me feel happy. Hey, I need to get going. Let's shoot some hoops at the community center one of these days. I'll look for your bikes. See you kids later."

That evening on the beach, the Bridgers and Poseys barbecued steak and corn on the cob. They used driftwood for their table and benches: smooth, white logs that had washed ashore. In the chilly air, they put on sweaters to watch the sunset. The lake turned pink, then purple, and soon, Lost Island was just a shadow.

"Ready to work?" Uncle Wyatt asked the kids. For safety, they were dousing the camp-fire with cups of water from the lake.

"Ready!" they answered. Flashlights on, they called their dogs, but Yum-Yum and Rascal didn't pay attention. The little poodle and terrier were chasing each other along the darkening beach, happy to run wild after being inside all day.

In Uncle Wyatt's driveway, he brought out his toolbox. By lantern light, he helped his daughter and nephews fix Sophie's bike. Tessie supervised the operation. The old yellow Lab sat among the tools, her front paw folded under her chest.

Finally, Uncle Wyatt gave the children rags to clean their hands. "The paint should be dry by now," he said.

Claire took the bike for a test drive to their front porch and back. "Yippee," she cried. "It works!"

"Okay, kids. Shall we call it a day?"

Claire rested the bike on its kickstand. "Daddy? Could we clean out our garage before we go to bed?"

"*Tonight?*" Uncle Wyatt pushed his sleeve up to look at his watch. "It's ten o'clock."

David said, "It won't take long, Uncle Wyatt."

"So why tonight and not tomorrow?"

"School starts in a couple days," said Jeff, "so we're kind of in a hurry. It's a personal matter."

Uncle Wyatt closed the lid of his toolbox and headed for the garage. "It won't take long, you say?"

"We'll be quick, Daddy."

16

The Ol' Switcheroo

The Blue Mountain Lodge looked out over the lake, its window boxes blooming with white and yellow daisies. The lobby was busy with families turning in room keys and carrying luggage out to their cars. Soon the town of Cabin Creek would be quiet again.

The cousins sat on the dock in front of the lodge, watching a fisherman in his small motorboat. A kayaker paddled toward the marina.

"I can't wait," Claire said, glancing over at their bikes and caboose, which was covered with a green tarp.

"Me, neither," said Jeff.

"Let's check one more time," David suggested.

The threesome pulled back the tarp. Underneath was the toaster Claire had bought for two dollars, a teakettle, and some pots and pans. There was a folding lawn chair and a radio. A small duffel bag bulged with the boys' collection of puzzles and monster transformers.

Rrrrrring . . . rrrrring! Rrrrrring . . . rrrrring! "Hey, guys!" called Sophie Garcia, thumbing the bell on her bike. She was nine years old. Her brown hair blew off her shoulders and her brown eyes were merry as she rode up to the dock. "I'm glad to see you again!"

"Same here!" the cousins cried.

The frame of Sophie's bicycle was still yellow, but the spokes of one wheel were now blue, the other purple. The handlebars swooped up with ribbons that fluttered in the breeze. Two new baskets were on either side of her rear fender, which had been painted green. It was a fine bike. The cousins had delivered it the day before, after phoning to make sure Sophie was back in town. They had been nervous to confess their story, but she surprised them.

"I'm not mad at you guys," she had said in her front yard. "This is the coolest bike I've ever seen. No one in Cabin Creek has one like it."

Now at the marina, Sophie parked by her friends.

"I'm ready," she said. "Do you have the address?"

"Right here." Jeff took a piece of paper from his pocket. "Corner of Elm and Maple, green house with white shutters. Mr. Fairmont said the family is staying there temporarily."

"So their cabin really burned to the ground?" Sophie asked.

"Yep. But no one got hurt," said David.

"Do you remember what you're supposed to say?" Claire asked the girl.

"I've been practicing in my head all morning. Trust me." Sophie flashed the peace sign, then a thumbs-up, their secret code meaning everything was cool.

"Okay," said Jeff. "Time for the ol' switcheroo." He patted the caboose, then helped Sophie climb up onto his taller bike. Claire then got on Sophie's because the girls were the same size, and Jeff took Claire's. Meanwhile David was on his own bike, trying to do a wheelie.

"Meet you back here for our picnic!" Sophie waved.

The cousins watched their friend ride along the lake path with their rattling cart. When she turned from the swimming beach toward the park, they began to follow — but at a distance, so no one would suspect they were together.

Now Sophie headed down Elm Street. When she came to Maple, she stopped at a green cottage and rang the doorbell.

On the opposite corner, the cousins hid under the spreading branches of a blue spruce.

"Hello, Mrs. Hartley," they heard Sophie say when a woman opened the door. "Special delivery!" Sophie pulled back the tarp.

"Oh!" cried the woman, pressing her hand to her heart. "This is . . . how did you know? You're so kind."

"Not me, ma'am. I'm just the driver, sent by some cheerful citizens of Cabin Creek."

"But who? I'd like to thank them."

"I'm sorry, but I'm not at liberty to say."

Under the spruce tree, Jeff, David, and Claire wiggled like puppies.

"Mrs. Hartley is happy!" Claire whispered.

"And she's carrying your toaster into the house," said Jeff.

"Look at her little kids," David said. "They like our toy monsters."

The cousins crawled out from under the tree. Without a word they got on their bikes and rode back to the marina.

The foursome sat on the dock eating peanut butter sandwiches. They dangled their feet over the water, enjoying the splash of tiny waves and the warm sunshine. They drank from their canteens.

For dessert, Sophie opened a box of Girl Scout cookies and passed them around. "Besides going back to school tomorrow, what's our next mission?" she asked.

Jeff looked at the sky, wondering about the weather. Puffy white clouds billowed over the mountains. "Sophie, we've been talking. If it doesn't rain next weekend, do you want to go camping with us? We can show you around Lost Island."

"Yeah!" she cried. "My grandparents bought me a sleeping bag and a compass. I am *so* ready to go exploring."

"We'll have a blast," said Claire. "There's no one around for miles and miles."

"No one around?" Sophie asked.

"Nope."

Sophie took a bite of her cookie, chewing slowly. "I've heard there're a lot of strange things out there."

The cousins nodded, then Jeff said, "It does seem that something always happens on Lost Island."

If you loved this mystery,
be sure to come back to

CABIN CREEK...

a small town with a lot of BIG secrets!

Read all of the

Turn the page for a sneak peek!

#1: THE SECRET OF ROBBER'S CAVE

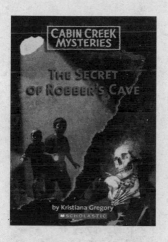

Lost Island was off limits — until now. Jeff and David are going to the deserted island to search for clues — and hidden treasure. Town legend tells of a robber and a secret cave, but the brothers have to piece the truth together. With the help of their cousin, Claire, they'll get to the bottom of the mystery, no matter what they have to dig up!

#2: The Clue at the Bottom of the Lake

It's the middle of the night when Jeff spots someone dumping a large bundle into the lake. It's too dark to identify anyone — or anything. But the cousins immediately suspect foul play, and plunge right into the mystery. Before they know it, the kids of Cabin Creek are in too deep. Everyone is a suspect — and the cousins are all in danger!

#3: The Legend of Skull Cliff

When a camper disappears from the dangerous lookout at Skull Cliff, the cousins wonder if it is the old town curse at work. Then the police discover a ransom note, and everyone is in search of a kidnapper. But Jeff, David, and Claire can't make the clues fit. Was the bossy boy from the city kidnapped, or did something even spookier take place on Skull Cliff?

#4: THE HAUNTING
OF HILLSIDE SCHOOL

When a girl's face appears, then disappears, outside a window of their spooky old schoolhouse, the cousins think they've seen a ghost. More strange clues — piano music lilting through empty halls, a secret passageway, and an old portrait that looks like the girl from the window — make Jeff, David, and Claire begin to wonder: Is their school just spooky, or could it be . . . haunted?

#5: THE BLIZZARD ON BLUE MOUNTAIN

Jeff, David, and Claire love their winter break jobs at the ski chalet on Blue Mountain, where they get to snowboard and sled between shifts. But when things start going missing from the chalet, the cousins find themselves prime suspects. Can they solve the mystery before they get ski-lifted out of their winter wonderland?

Meet the Kreeps

Check out the whole spooky series!

#1: There Goes the Neighborhood

#2: The New Step-Mummy

#3: The Nanny Nightmare

#4: The Mad Scientist